The Others

Book 3

D0596268

My New Normal

Sara Michelle

SADDLEBACK℠
EDUCATIONAL PUBLISHING

My New Normal

The Aftermath * Book 1
The Inside * Book 2
The Others * Book 3

SADDLEBACK ℠
EDUCATIONAL PUBLISHING
www.sdlback.com

ISBN-13: 978-1-61651-772-4
ISBN-10: 1-61651-772-7
eBook: 978-1-61247-352-9

Printed in Guangzhou, China
0911/CA21101549

16 15 14 13 12   1 2 3 4 5

Day 14

9:55 a.m.

When I was in fourth grade, I was tormented by the class bully, Jeffery Hugh. He was a husky kid with bright orange hair and freckles everywhere. He always told me that I was stupid or fat. But what hurt me the most was when he told me that when the world ended, I was going to be the only one left behind. I never thought that he would be right.

My thoughts drifted back to the events of last night. I remember Renee coming in to wish us a good night's sleep. And I remember snuggling with Ryan and getting ready to fall asleep. Then we heard the scream. I was completely terrified. We were defenseless.

When we opened the door, the screaming continued. Ryan grabbed the lamp. I was honestly terrified. I knew Ryan was too because when I grabbed his hand, it was shaking. If you think rationally, it was ridiculous for teenagers to deal with this kind of threat. We'd already witnessed the world falling to pieces. We'd lost everyone and everything we loved. We'd both been dreadfully ill. Who knew what was going to hit us next?

We followed the scream, and it led us into the living area with the two couches and broken TV. We peeked around the corner and what we saw made my stomach seize. Renee was facing Jason. She was talking madly and gesturing wildly. I didn't realize why until I saw what Jason was holding in his hand. One of the butcher knives from the kitchen was firmly in his right hand. His face looked smug, slightly annoyed, and almost threatening. Renee continued her ranting.

"Who the *hell* do you think you are, walking around like some crazed man with a knife in your hand? This is supposed to be a place of refuge! There are children here!" she continued on.

Ryan squeezed my hand. He put

down the lamp before walking out of
the kitchen and toward the pair.

"Ryan, no!" I whispered loudly. He
shook his head and continued forward.
I wanted to cry. We had no idea how
crazy Jason could be. I wished I'd
listened to Ryan when he voiced his
suspicions earlier.

"Hey, guys what's going on here?"
Ryan asked quietly.

Renee turned and looked at Ryan.
Her face was a pale and her eyes were
dilated.

"I come out of the bedroom to get
some water from the kitchen, and I
find this man walking around here
with a butcher knife! He claims to be
on the lookout. But he fails to realize
that there is nothing in the world to

lookout for," she huffed.

I watched Ryan take a deep breath and turn his head toward Jason.

"What the heck are you doing, man? There are kids here. You'd scare them if they saw you," Ryan said.

Jason laughed. "Maybe that's the point!"

Renee and Ryan looked at each other worriedly. They looked back at Jason. He rolled his eyes.

"God, I'm kidding. I just want to keep a lookout on the place. In case some wild survivor comes barging in. Or an animal. Or God knows what," Jason snarked.

Renee's anger returned. "The only wild survivor to be fearful of is you!" She pointed a finger at his chest and gave him a shove.

I had to give her props, she definitely had guts. But then again, after all we'd been through the past few weeks, what was one more deadly threat?

Jason glared at Renee. That's when Ryan decided to get between them. He put his hands on both Renee and Jason. I could tell that he was aggravated.

"Jason, I don't care how old or big you are. I knew you were trouble the minute I met you. We found this shelter. It's my responsibility. And it's under my control. I can't have you walking around the shelter with a weapon. I don't care what you say you're doing it for," Ryan stated.

At this Jason began chuckling. First a soft giggle, and then a loud laugh.

"Kid, you slay me. I felt that from the moment I laid eyes on you." Shaking his head, he handed the knife to Ryan and began to walk down the hallway toward me. I pressed my back against the kitchen wall, praying he wouldn't see me.

"Where do you think you're going?" Ryan yelled.

I gasped. I'd never heard Ryan raise his voice like that before. I peeked around the corner and saw Jason stop in his tracks. He slowly turned his head around to face Ryan again. I gulped. I was just glad that Ryan had the knife now.

"Excuse me?" Jason almost whispered.

I began to shake. Ryan was pushing

it. That I could tell.

Ryan met Jason's tone and whispered back, "I said, where do you think you're going?"

Jason didn't move for a moment. It seemed like he was trying to decide what to say to Ryan.

"Well, I was planning on going back to my room to sleep since nobody needs my help out here."

Ryan shook his head. "I don't think so."

Jason laughed nervously. "What are you going to do? Stab me?"

Renee gave Ryan a look that indicated that she didn't seem to think stabbing Jason was a bad idea. I knew Ryan didn't have the guts to do it. And if he did, then I didn't really know him like I thought I did.

"I am not a murderer. But I want you to leave the shelter," Ryan said.

I dropped my jaw. It was the middle of the night. It was freezing outside. There was nothing. And there was nowhere to go. I almost wanted to admit that stabbing him was probably kinder than sending him away.

Jason crossed his arms over his chest. He resembled a child who had just been given a timeout.

"You can't make me leave, kid," he said firmly. There was uncertainty in his voice.

Ryan held up the knife threateningly. "Oh really?"

I wanted to laugh. Where were the cameras? Were we in a bad movie?

Jason shook his head. "You're really going to make me leave? Where am I supposed to go?" he whined.

Ryan lowered the knife. He wasn't a mean person. But Jason really posed a threat to all of us. We all had received an "I'm crazy" vibe from him.

"Look, Jason, it's not that I want to send you out there. Now I have to think about everyone's safety, not just my own. We can't have you here with us," Ryan stated.

Jason shook his head. "You're a heartless kid. You really are. Do I get to keep the knife to protect myself with?"

"Protect yourself against what? No way, man. You are on your own."

Jason shook his head. "All right kid, whatever. I'll get out of your hair for now. But this doesn't mean I won't be back. Remember that," he threatened.

Ignoring his threat, I tiptoed over to the pantry and grabbed two water bottles and some crackers. Taking a deep breath, I walked out of the kitchen and toward Renee and Ryan who were walking Jason toward the stairs.

"Jason, wait," I said.

Ryan and Renee stopped and turned around. They looked bewildered.

Then Jason turned around too. Anger glistened in his eyes, but I could also see fear. I really did feel bad for him.

"I thought you may want this stuff. Just in case you can't find anything else," I mumbled.

"What is this? Some pity gift?" he asked, snatching the supplies out of my hand.

I put my head down and looked at the floor. I felt horrible, I really did. But it just didn't seem safe with him here.

"Don't treat my girlfriend like that," Ryan said sternly. "You don't deserve the food and water. Just take the gift and leave. I don't want to see you back here again."

"You know you're going to regret this, kid," Jason said as he stomped up the stairs with Ryan following behind.

After he exited, Ryan bolted the door. The three of us stood in silence for a moment.

Renee spoke first. "Well, I'm glad we took care of that problem," she stated blankly.

"Do you think he'll come back?" I asked nervously. It seemed unlikely to think a man of that size would actually listen to us.

"Probably," Ryan muttered.

I shivered. I hated knowing that we had no one to rely on but ourselves. There was no 911. We really were all alone.

"I think we should all get some sleep. It's late," Renee said, rubbing her arms.

"I agree," I said, and walked up to Ryan to grab his hand.

He let me put my hand in his, and we silently walked back to our bedroom. He was really quiet.

"Ryan, are you okay?" I asked. "He's gone. It's okay," I soothed.

"It's really not okay, Cecilia," he said in disgust. "He could've killed someone. And I would've been responsible for it. I knew we shouldn't have let him join us in the first place. But no, you had to convince me to let him take refuge here."

My jaw dropped. So *this* was my fault? "Babe, I didn't even—"

"No! Don't call me babe right now, Cecilia." He ran his fingers through his hair and sighed. He then walked over to the bed and flopped down.

I was pissed. "Excuse me? At least I still have a heart! This disaster has left you cold, Ryan."

I saw Ryan shake his head. His back was turned to me, and he made no effort to acknowledge me.

"Ryan, you're acting like a child. Look at me," I said. He didn't. "I'm sleeping somewhere else tonight." I was so annoyed.

I ended up sleeping on the couch. As I drifted off, I felt truly alone. The memories haunted me. When I closed my eyes the first things I saw were flashing lights and the earth trembling beneath my feet. I saw the fear that was etched onto Ryan's face right before I blacked out. It was terrifying. Those memories would never leave me.

Memories of my mom filled my head. Tears welled in my eyes. I missed her so much. The day of the quake, the moms had gone out New Year's Eve shopping. They were hoping to catch last-minute bargains. Our families were throwing a party. I wondered what happened to them. A small part inside of me hoped that maybe they were still alive, but I knew the chances were slim.

Then I really began crying. This new normal sucked. I wanted my mother. I wanted my family. I wanted to go to school. I wanted my bed. I wanted a McFlurry. Pizza. French fries. Tacos. But here I was sleeping alone on a strange couch in a snow shelter that I never gave a second thought. My boyfriend was angry. And Jason could come back whenever … Life sucked. I'd had enough.

I woke up to the vague smell of oatmeal. I never liked oatmeal.

Day 14

10:15 a.m.

In the kitchen Renee, Brittany, and
Henry were sitting at the table eating—surprise, surprise—oatmeal. My
stomach rumbled and I walked over to
scoop my own bowl. I silently ate my
oatmeal and listened in. Renee was tell-
ing everyone what went down last night.

"Sweetheart, I know last night was
rough," Renee said, walking over and
putting her hand on my shoulder. "But
I don't think that man will be coming

back around here again. And if he does, I'm not afraid to pull the knife. Did you sleep okay last night?"

I looked up at her and tried to smile. It probably came out looking more like a wince. "I slept fine, Renee. Thank you," I muttered.

She gave me a sympathetic smile. I felt slightly annoyed. It was going to be one of those days. I could already tell. I was a grump. I lost my appetite, so I got up and rinsed off my bowl.

I walked out of the kitchen and stood in the hallway debating whether or not to peek in on Ryan. I'd never had to think like this before. And it confused me. It hurt too. I felt dumb standing there. So I decided to go back into the kitchen, but suddenly Ryan walked out of our room. I stiffened and tried to remind myself that this was Ryan. He didn't stay mad. He never even got mad. This was probably some freak misunderstanding. I smiled at him. He gave me a weird look. Oh. My. God. He was still pissed.

"Cecilia, now is not a good time to talk about things. Right now, I need to figure out a way to go find more resources for all of us. We aren't going to be able to hold off much longer."

My shoulders slumped. Why was he acting so cold? I hadn't intentionally done anything to hurt him. I was just trying to do the right thing. Jason *had* rescued five people. He guided them to the shelter. Didn't that mean anything?

"Ryan, I'm sorry," I whispered.

I bowed my head. I expected him to come over and at least tell me I was forgiven. But when I looked up he was staring at me blankly.

"Cecilia, there isn't anything to be sorry for. Stop apologizing all the time. Is all the breakfast gone?" he asked.

My jaw dropped. When did my mature Ryan become a surly and unfamiliar teenager? Ryan was supposed to be different. He was supposed to be a gentleman. But he was just being an ass.

"Why are you acting so weird, Ryan?" I asked timidly. I was afraid of his answer.

He sighed and shook his head. "I just have a lot to figure out, Cecilia. Try to give me a break," he snapped.

I was so confused as he walked away. Here I was, all by myself in the middle of the hallway. I just didn't get it. When did he morph into a moody, grouchy guy? Where did my normal boyfriend disappear to?

I wanted to cry, but I knew that wouldn't help anything. Crying was for wimps. I didn't want to cry more than I already had. It was getting old. I decided I needed to find something to occupy my time until Ryan got over his mood swing.

I walked back to couch in the living room. I had no idea what to do with myself. Ryan obviously had everything under control. Whatever that meant. I sighed. I tried to think of ways that I could help around the shelter. Maybe

I could be the cruise director, organizing activities for everyone to pass the time? So lame, I decided.

I groaned. I felt like I was some helpless, annoying princess who couldn't do anything without bothering someone. I needed to suck it up. But hey, at least my cold seemed to have disappeared overnight. Maybe it was my body processing the grief, just like I thought.

I thought about Jason. How was he handling things? Deep down I really did feel bad for kicking him out. But something was off about him. Even I had to admit that.

I lay back down on the couch and kept thinking through everything that had happened over the past 24 hours.

Ryan and I had been completely fine yesterday. Why did one scary situation make him mad at me? It just wasn't like him at all. I wanted to cry. Again. But I was being an idiot. I had to grow up. This wasn't helping anything. We all had way bigger things to be worrying about. So I marched off to take a shower and try to get a new start on my day.

Day 14

10:50 a.m.

As the warm water ran down my body, I once again began thinking about times before the world had caved in on itself. I remembered how Ryan would come over so many mornings to cook breakfast with my mom. Once the food was ready my mom would let Ryan wake me up. He'd wake me up a different way nearly every time he came over. We had so many funny memories of the stupid things he'd do to wake me up. One morning he tickled me with a feather. He stood above me and tickled my face with that feather until I wanted to smack him. Another time he got the local DJ to play my favorite song on the radio. When I would finally roll out of bed, he'd greet me with a bear hug. No kissing until I brushed my teeth. Ew.

He was the boyfriend of any girl's dreams. He was smart. And he was popular in school. But he was never mean to anyone. He was way better than me. Gorgeous, kind, charming, hilarious, and our moms were best friends. We were kind of like one big happy family. I'd give anything to go back. No amount of pinching could change the facts though. This was not a dream. This was real. And I didn't have anyone to help me get through it. Who could I talk to? Who wasn't suffering the same fate? It killed me how our lives were forever changed. Every morning, for what seemed like forever, I would wake up remembering that we were living this nightmare.

I kept myself from crying and dried myself off. In the mirror I stared at the reflection looking back at me. My hair had seemed to grow longer. It hung well past my shoulders and was kind of wavy. My cheeks were bright red from the heat of the shower. My eyes seemed to sparkle against my super white skin. I felt like I looked completely different. I'd never gone this long without wearing makeup or styling my hair. I guess I will never use mascara or a flat iron again. But wow, I looked relaxed and completely at peace. This was the 100% complete opposite of what I was feeling inside. Inside, I felt emotionally raw and vulnerable. Did Ryan hate how I looked now? Is that why he was so weird? I shook my head. That wasn't it. He wasn't superficial.

Day 14

11:10 a.m.

I left the bathroom and put my clothes back on. I was really getting tired of wearing sweats and a big T-shirt. I felt boyish and out of my skin. But it's not like I had much of a choice. I hated to sound stuck up, but I was sick of not having choices. I missed shopping, and going out to dinner, and seeing my friends. I missed my car. I missed pretty clothes. I even missed AP Chemistry. I missed Ryan wanting to be with me. My heart ached. Nothing was right.

Just when I was about to lose it again, someone knocked on my door. My heart began beating faster and butterflies twirled in my stomach. It felt wrong. I hadn't felt this nervous about seeing Ryan in months. He always made me feel just right. Why did I have to worry about him now?

I coughed and tried to straighten my shirt. That's when I realized no matter how much I straightened it, it'd still be the same baggy old T-shirt I'd been wearing. I sighed and walked over to open the door. When I did, it wasn't exactly who I was hoping for, but it was good enough.

Little Daniel stood before me with a shy grin on his face. I smiled. This little boy had to be the cutest thing I'd ever seen.

"Cecilia, I'm bored," he said shyly. My heart went out to him. He was all alone. His parents were gone. And his entire normal habitat had been demolished. I decided that Daniel was going to be the distraction I needed from my love life.

I kneeled down. "You're bored?" I cried in an overly enthusiastic voice. "How is that possible? This place is full of things to do!"

He giggled, unaware of the large amount of sarcasm in my voice. I picked him up and carried him over to my bed. I threw him on to my pillows where he laughed cheerfully.

"Let's make up a game!" I cried, throwing myself onto the bed with him. It felt nice to be fooling around like a kid again.

Daniel sat back up and crossed his legs on my bed. He stared at me curiously.

"What kind of game?" he asked.

I thought a moment. What were the games I used to play with my mom as a kid? I browsed through the memories in my brain until I finally decided on the alphabet game. My mom and I used to play it when I was younger. On car rides, before I went to sleep, and even when I was in timeout, we'd play. I looked at Daniel and my heart reached out toward him. His entire life had been completely altered. But he was still a child. He looked at the world with innocence and curiosity.

"Have you ever played the alphabet game?" I asked him.

His face lit up. "We used to play that in preschool! I'm really, really good at it, Cecilia!"

I laughed. The alphabet game was a game where the first person starts off saying A is for … and named an object that started with A. The game would continue on. But every time you added a letter, you had to go and repeat the letters and objects that were named before it.

"Okay, Daniel, you start!" I exclaimed.

He jumped up and down on the bed and excitedly began the game.

"A is for …" He scrunched his face up and thought a moment.

I was somewhat jealous. I wished I was able to forget all my problems as easily as he did.

"Apple!" he cried.

I laughed. All that thought, and that's what he'd come up with.

"My turn," I said. "A is for apple. B is for …" I pretended to put a lot of thought into my answer. I decided to keep it easy for him. "Book!" I said.

"My turn now! A is for apple. B is for book. And C is for clothes," he giggled. "Because you can't possibly do anything naked!" He laughed hysterically.

His laughter made me laugh. I missed having the innocence he so proudly held.

We continued our game, and I found myself forgetting about Ryan and all of my other problems. But as soon as our game got stuck on the letter X, we heard a knock on my door. *Whoosh*! All my problems came rushing back.

I stood up and nervously brushed my wrinkled sweats and tried to redo my hair. It didn't do much good. Vanity was worthless in this new reality. I slowly walked over to the door and took a deep breath before opening it.

Day 14

Noon

It was Ryan. My heart raced.

"Hey," I muttered, looking at the ground. I was too embarrassed and still a little miffed to look at him.

"Hey, Daniel is in here, right? Renee was worried," he said.

I nodded. But why would Renee care?

"Okay," he said pausing. He was looking at me, and I didn't want to look him in the eye. It was too hard. "We should talk," he said quietly.

I peered up at him. He was now staring at the ground also. This was one of those awkward moments where I had absolutely no idea what to say. I was almost never at a loss for words.

"I agree," I muttered.

I looked behind me. Daniel was sitting on the bed staring at us curiously. His head was turned to the right slightly, and his eyes were wide with questions. He looked like a little puppy.

I gave him a smile to reassure him. Everything was going to be okay, my smile said. Don't worry, my smile said. You'll be taken care of, my smile said. I turned back to look at Ryan. He was staring at me so hard that I blushed. I didn't know whether this was one of those really sweet moments or really awkward moments.

"Let's go talk now," he insisted.

"What about Daniel?" I asked.

"Daniel can go be with Renee for a little bit. Hey, Daniel, can you come here real quick?" Ryan asked him.

Daniel jumped off the bed and shuffled his feet over to the door. He looked up at me and took my hand in his. He was so freakin' cute.

"Daniel, I need to talk to Ryan about a few things right now. I'll come get you in a little bit. Let's go see Renee and Brittany and Michael," I said to him gently.

Daniel nodded. Seeing his little fingers grasp my hand was heartbreaking. It all was so unfair. Daniel was an orphan. I was an orphan.

"Ryan, I'm going to take him to Renee. I'll meet you here in a few minutes," I declared firmly.

Ryan nodded and leaned against the door. I walked with Daniel down the hall. I found Renee in the living room sitting with Michael and Henry. Brittany was nowhere to be seen.

"Hey, Renee, would you mind watching Daniel for a little bit? I need to go talk to Ryan about a couple things," I asked.

Renee smiled. "Of course, dear! Come here, schnooks!" she cooed to Daniel.

He gave me a strange look. Then he rolled his eyes. I almost laughed but instead handed Daniel over to Renee.

I felt bad for him because I sensed that Renee would baby him too much, but I had to talk to Ryan.

I gave him a reassuring look before returning to Ryan. I stood in front of the bedroom door for a few minutes. I was trying to catch my breath and collect my thoughts. We had to fix this. Without him I wasn't going to be able to do any of this. It was hard enough being here without my family, but without him I would truly have nothing. That was not an option.

After a few moments, I took one last deep breath and turned the doorknob. I slowly walked inside and was surprised to find that he wasn't on the bed or anywhere to be seen in the room. I sighed. I was annoyed. Then

I realized the water was running. Once again I was just overreacting. Drama. Queen.

"Cecilia, one second, I hopped in the shower!" I heard him say.

I walked over and sat on the bed trying to figure out the worst case scenario of the discussion that was about to go down. The worst thing he could do was the obvious—dump me. I swallowed. That would suck. I'd never been dumped. I didn't know how someone—especially the guy I thought I knew like the back of my hand—could dump me. Especially now, at the end of days. I mean in all honesty, what were the other options?. Unless he decided to make a move on Brittany ... That would be gross.

Just as I was about to give up and leave the room, Ryan opened the bathroom door. He stood there wrapped in a towel. His ripped chest radiated steam, and his dripping wet hair hung past his ears. His eyes glistened. His beard was scruffy and masculine. Then I really debated on whether or not to leave the room. He was smokin'. Stunning. And next to him I'm sure I looked like something the cat dragged in.

Looking like a Greek god wasn't going to help the whole "working things out" deal either. I sighed. My mouth gaped open. I looked at him. His eyes never left mine. I felt uncomfortable, which was a feeling completely foreign to me. Especially where Ryan was involved. We'd had the s-e-x talk many times. I wasn't ready. He was totally cool about it.

I looked down at my fingernails and tears welled in my eyes. I couldn't imagine being without him. I tried to control my breathing and remain calm. All he wanted to do was talk. What's the worst thing that could possibly happen? I already knew. If I could survive the apocalypse, then I could survive being dumped. Right?

I heard him sigh. Clearly he was irritated. "Cecilia, why aren't you looking at me? We need to talk," he said.

I wanted to say, "Ryan, put on some clothes. Do you realize how hot you are in that towel? It's *very* distracting." But I just shrugged my shoulders. I slowly raised my head and looked at him. But he'd gone back into the bathroom and closed the door. Hopefully he was putting on some clothes.

I tried to remind myself once again that this was Ryan. My Ryan. This wasn't some gorgeous stranger who just happened to want to talk with me.

When Ryan reappeared, dressed, I had finally composed myself. I was chill. If he was going to dump me, then I was going to act as if I didn't care. He walked over to the bed and sat down.

"Cecilia," he sighed. My breathing quickened. He took my hand and placed it in his.

"Look at me," he whispered. I raised my head up. We were eye to eye. Just when I thought I was going to puke from all the butterflies, my breathing returned to normal. I finally stopped shaking. I found my place in his eyes. I forgot the fighting and the nervousness and relaxed. I was home.

"What did *I* do wrong?" I asked.

He shook his head. "Nothing at all, I'm just trying to figure everything out. I'm so sorry. I feel responsible for everyone. I knew Jason was bad news, but I didn't follow my gut. I was *really* mad at myself."

To tell the truth, I felt a little righteous. My confidence was restored. I was tired of the pity party.

He lightly kissed me on the lips. My heart was back to normal. This was just what I needed. He gave me the strength to believe everything would be okay. We'd made it so far together.

And it seemed like no matter what the problem, we could fix it. We were a team. Without each other, I'm not sure what would go down. We sat there in silence looking into each others eyes. He took a deep breath.

Day 14

12:25 p.m.

"We need to talk though," he stated.

My stomach dropped. What? Seriously! What could he possibly need to say now?

"What's up?" I muttered, taking his hand in mine.

He sighed. "Henry and I were talking. We're not going to be able to last on supplies here for much longer. We've five extra people here. We have to start looking for more food. Doing that means

I need to leave for a couple days."

I closed my eyes. He was going out there again. It hit me then that I hadn't been outside since we'd arrived. It'd been days. How did it look? Was there more snow? I wondered if any more survivors were going to be found. I wondered if Ryan would be safe. I had so many questions. I also had a million reasons why he shouldn't leave. But I knew it was right. I knew we were running short. And I knew our lives depended on finding more supplies and keeping the shelter up and running.

"For how long?" I asked.

He shrugged his shoulders. "It's hard to say. Depends on how far we have to travel and what problems we run into along the way. Don't forget how long it took to walk here through all of the destruction."

How could I forget it? How could I forget the people we saw along the way? They were burned into my brain. My hands began to shake. He couldn't risk his life like this. Why couldn't just Henry and Michael go? Michael was older than Ryan. He should suck it up and take it into his own hands. I knew what I thinking wasn't right, and I knew Ryan needed to go. But I wanted to be with him.

"Let me come," I pleaded. But I knew that he would argue that I wasn't strong enough to go.

He shook his head. "Babe, you're not going with me. You are way too slow. Plus you need to stay here with the girls and Daniel. You guys will be fine, I promise. And I'll come back as soon as I can, I swear to you."

I wanted to cry … again. I felt like such a wimp.

"When are you guys leaving?" I sniffed.

"Tomorrow morning," he answered flatly.

Then the tears really filled my eyes. Why so soon?

"That soon?" I asked.

I bawled like a little girl. I cried so hard that I gave myself hiccups. I didn't want him to leave. I felt like a little baby, but the past 24 hours had been so overwhelming. My vow of no more tears was toast.

He held me while I cried. We must have sat there for, like, ten minutes in silence. Well, except for my blubbering. And the hiccups. After I calmed myself down, I faced him. I knew I must have looked vile. Snotty nose. Red eyes. Great.

"It will all be okay, Cecilia. I swear this is just what has to happen. This is what it's going to be like now. I know it sucks. But I have to be one of the adults now. There's no one else but us. We don't have our moms running to the market when we're out of bread. The things we took for granted before are in our hands now."

He sounded so much older, and on a completely different level than I was.

All I could do was nod. I didn't have a choice. He was going to have to leave. When was I going to grow up?

Day 14

12:40 p.m.

I was exhausted. Crying really drains you. It's not recommended. I tried to look perky. But I was pretty sure Ryan could tell because he kissed my forehead and suggested that I take a nap.

"Take one with me," I whispered, tracing the veins on his hand. I just wanted one last nap with him before he left.

"Babe, I have a lot of stuff to do before tomorrow, I don't really have time for a nap."

I looked at him pleadingly with my eyes. He sighed and gave in.

"Just a short nap," he said.

I smiled and nodded. He got up and pulled the covers back and climbed into bed. I scooted right beside him. I turned to look him in the eyes, and he put his hands around my waist.

"I'm so sorry about being a jerk last night," he whispered.

I smiled. I didn't even care as long as we were okay now.

"It's all right. You were just having a rough time," I replied.

"I love you," he stated.

"And I love you," I whispered back, kissing his forehead.

"Get some sleep. I'll be here when you wake up," he said.

I snuggled in closer to him and fell into a relaxing sleep.

Day 14

6:45 p.m.

I woke up feeling completely relaxed. I had made myself sick over our non-existent breakup. But the pain in my heart that had been bugging me for the past day disappeared. I felt at ease with Ryan's arms still holding me in a tight embrace. I sighed. I really wished he didn't have to leave.

I turned around to face him. He was still sleeping. His hair hung in front of his face, and his lips were slightly parted. He looked so cute that I almost didn't want to wake him up. I wondered what time it was. I felt like we'd slept for a while. Right when I decided to wake him up, his eyes opened.

I was embarrassed that he'd caught me watching him sleep.

"Cecilia, what are you doing?" he asked, stretching. "Were you watching me sleep?"

"I don't know. You looked so peaceful. I didn't know whether to wake you up or not," I admitted.

He laughed. "You're such a stalker," he said playfully.

I smiled. I was so glad we were okay now.

"How late is it?" he asked.

I shrugged my shoulders. "Do I look like a clock?" I asked sarcastically.

He squinted his eyes. "Kind of," he replied.

I slapped him jokingly on the arm. He smiled and gave me a peck on the cheek.

We lay there for a few more minutes before Ryan broke the silence.

"I'm hungry, babe. Let's go eat." He slightly pushed me away from him and rolled off the bed. He readjusted his shirt and flipped his hair back. I loved when he did that.

I straightened my frumpy T-shirt. Then I threw my hair back into a ponytail and took his hand as we walked out of the bedroom. I was surprised that the clocks read almost seven. That meant it was getting so much closer to morning, which is when Ryan would be leaving along with Henry and Michael. I clenched his hand tighter in mine. He gave it a reassuring squeeze.

We walked into the kitchen where Renee was making food. Brittany and Daniel were sitting at the table.

"Hey, kids!" Renee said enthusiastically, as always.

I smiled. I knew that she was faking the enthusiasm for the sake of the kids.

"Hey, Renee. Whatcha making?" Ryan asked.

Before she could answer my stomach loudly announced its hunger. Embarrassing. Ryan looked at me and started laughing. Dainty sounds these were not.

"Hopefully something yummy ... Cecilia's having some stomach issues right now," he joked.

I playfully shoved him and laughed. I really was starving.

"Well, it looks like we're having peanut butter sandwiches tonight. You actually get the opportunity to choose chunky or smooth!" Renee advertised both kinds of spread.

"I think I'm going to have to go with chunky." Ryan lifted his shirt and patted his nonexistent tummy fat.

"Smooth all the way," I stated.

Renee laughed, "Making it so difficult kids!"

I walked over and sat down at the table with Brittany and Daniel.

"Sorry about cutting our game short,

Daniel," I told him.

Brittany smiled. "He's fine, Cecilia. We picked up where you guys left off. Well, actually we started over, but you know what I mean."

"I beat her twice, Cecilia!" Daniel exclaimed.

I looked at Brittany, and she winked at me. I smiled. Everyone was trying to make Daniel forget how awful our situation was …

"That's awesome, Daniel! You're a pro!" I said.

He grinned. I could see a little of his old self beneath the sadness.

Renee brought over our sandwich plates, and we all started to eat.

"I love peanut butter," Renee said, taking a bite out of her sandwich.

I didn't know what it was about her, but Renee really annoyed me. I gave Ryan a look, and he winked at me. She was trying to be upbeat and all, but … Sometimes perky people just suck the fun right out of a room.

"I loooove peanut butter too!" Ryan exclaimed taking a huge bite of his sandwich. He started smacking and chewing with his mouth open. Everyone laughed.

For a few moments we all sat there eating in silence. Then Henry and Michael walked in. I felt awkward since I hadn't had much of a conversation with either of them since they'd arrived. I'm sure that they thought that I was some kind of prima donna. I felt somewhat cold toward them too since they were the ones going with Ryan in the morning. I knew it was wrong since they were also risking their lives. But it was just hard to deal.

"Ah! Peanut butter sandwiches," Henry stated, rubbing his hands together.

Renee hopped up out of her seat. "I am a short order cook today. Let me make you boys a sandwich!"

"Why thank you, ma'am," Henry said, pretending to tip a hat at her. He sat down.

Michael didn't say a word and sat down next to Henry.

I continued eating and wondered if they were going to bring up their departure in front of Renee. Or did she already know?

"What time do you boys plan on leaving tomorrow morning?" Renee asked, setting plates down for both guys.

Question answered! She knew. I was way out of the loop.

Henry took a deep breath and took a large bite of his sandwich.

"I'm going to guess early. I want to get back to safety as soon as we can," he said while devouring his sandwich.

I winced. Losing all of the guys would be tragic. Because all of us girls—and Daniel—would be basically screwed. I didn't have much confidence in our survival skills.

"Where do you think we're going to find the additional food and supplies?" Michael asked.

Michael spoke! It was one of the only times I'd heard him speak to the group.

"I have no idea, honestly," Henry stated. "I didn't see much when Jason found us and brought us here. But I think we should stick with our plan. It's the best idea we've come up with so far."

"Yeah," Ryan said. "That part of town may have something to offer."

I was barely aware of the conversation. My stomach dropped. I'd forgotten about Jason. What would we do if he decided to show up while the guys were gone? Had Renee even considered this? Had any of them?

"What if Jason comes back?" I asked. I was panicking.

Everyone stopped and looked at me. Apparently Jason had turned into the "man who shall not be named." It was silent for a moment, and then Renee decided to be the big kid in the room and break the silence.

"If Jason comes back, I'll handle him. There's no reason to worry the boys anymore than they already are. They're being brave enough to go on this search for us. We'll handle whatever comes our way," she stated firmly.

I glared at her. Why did she always have to try to fix everything? I wasn't about to try and fight off Jason, so if Renee wanted to handle that, that'd be fine by me.

"I don't think Jason will be coming back. He didn't have any food or water, so he probably won't last very long," I said.

Renee and Ryan glared at me. That's when I remembered that I'd given him crackers and water. Duh.

"Well, I'm sure we'll be fine, either way," I muttered.

Day 14

7:15 p.m.

Right when things had begun to get kind of awkward, we heard a knock on the door. My stomach dropped. Was he back for revenge? Already?

"Perfect timing," Renee said, standing up. "I'll handle this."

We all watched her walk out of the kitchen. It was weird how nobody bothered to get up and follow her. A few minutes had passed, and she hadn't returned. What if Jason had returned and kidnapped her? Or even worse ... killed her? Right when I actually had begun to worry, she showed up in the doorway of the kitchen.

"Henry, Ryan, I think you guys better come check this out." She motioned them with her hands.

Why couldn't we come? I looked at Ryan questioningly. He shook his head slightly, indicating that I should stay where I was.

I obeyed. Henry and Ryan walked out of the kitchen and followed Renee up the stairs to the basement doors. Michael, Brittany, and I gave each other questioning looks as we tried to eavesdrop on the muffled conversations coming from the top steps. Minutes passed and nobody returned.

"I wonder if it's the FBI or something," Michael stated.

"I don't think so," I replied.

After a couple more minutes passed, we heard the front doors slam. The sound of the secured deadbolt was reassuring. Footsteps pounded back toward the kitchen. We all sat quietly. What was going to happen now?

We turned and looked in the doorway. Ryan, Henry, and Renee were standing there talking. But I was surprised to see a new guy standing there with them. He was a big, sturdy man with a long white beard and small blue eyes. I looked at Ryan curiously.

Ryan cleared his throat. "Guys, this is Dr. Jenkins. He has some pretty interesting stuff to say," Ryan said.

Dr. Jenkins let out a loud, hearty laugh.

Renee smiled and said, "Dr. Jenkins, why don't you take a seat?"

It was getting super weird.

"Why thank you, Renee, mighty kind of you," Dr. Jenkins boomed.

Daniel looked at me worriedly. The loud voice apparently had scared him.

"Want to come sit in my lap?" I whispered. He nodded and got up out of his chair. I picked him up and set him in my lap. I hugged him firmly.

Everyone sat down and looked at Dr. Jenkins. He took off his heavy coat. He was well-protected against the elements. Either he got lucky and found his warm clothes or … His beard was muddy. And he had a long cut on his right arm that was caked with dried blood. Although he looked physically like he should be in pain, his eyes and facial expressions said otherwise. He looked happy and thankful to be alive. He looked like a glass-half-full type of person. His eyes twinkled with a sense of humor. Maybe he knew of some inside joke that we didn't know about.

We all sat down and looked at each other awkwardly for a few moments.

"Well," Ryan started. "Dr. Jenkins is going to be joining us here at the shelter for a while, till we figure some more things out."

We all looked at him and waited for him to talk. I wondered what "interesting" things he had to say.

Day 14

7:30 p.m.

Dr. Jenkins cleared his throat and smiled. "Well, er, I'm not very good at introductions. But I'm Dr. Karl Jenkins. I'm a scientist of geological anomalies. I've been working with a small group of other scientists for about 20 years. We were all together when the earthquake struck. I'm the only one left. My partner, Dr. Fernando Gonzales, was with me up until yesterday. He was already pretty sick before the disaster, so he was lucky to have lasted as long as he did."

We all shifted in our chairs. Where was this leading?

"Anyway," he continued, "our group was only known to a few people. We were handled by a special unit of our government—an off-the-books unit. Another group of scientists in Rome knew about us too. We've been working for years. And we've been forecasting and anticipating this disaster for about 15 years. The truth is we had no idea that it was going to happen as quickly as it did. If we had, we would have notified the various authorities. We … or I should say I … know a lot about what's to come."

I think everyone in the room was shocked into complete silence. Everyone stared at this man. We were dumbfounded. I glanced at Ryan who now had his head in his hands. Renee continued staring at Dr. Jenkins. She hadn't moved once. Even Daniel didn't dare to squirm in my lap.

I swallowed. This man could hold some of the answers that we'd been searching for. He looked at us all as if he'd half expected our reaction. I shook my head slowly. I couldn't decide whether I was really excited or super pissed that Dr. Jenkins could've saved billions of lives but didn't. I had no idea what was going to come next or where we were all going to go from here. But what I did know was that we needed to brace ourselves—because from what I could tell we were about to learn that we were in for one hell of a crazy ride.

About the Author

Sara Michelle

As a high school student, I never thought that I could pursue my creative interests. But with the support of my family, I auditioned to attend an arts magnet program in south-central Texas. I'm so excited to be going to a school that lets me explore my right brain and harnesses my imagination.

Speaking of interests ... those would involve: singing, songwriting, dancing, reading, going out with friends, spending money, and—writing. I love this time in my life and plan to live it up while doing what I used to believe was impossible, writing and publishing books. One day I'd love to get my PhD in psychology—and in a parallel universe, I'd love to be an actor. My favorite food is ice cream; I could honestly live off of it 24/7. My friends mean the world to me, and I'd be absolutely nowhere without my large, crazy family. I can't wait to see what life has to offer, and I plan on enjoying every minute of it!

My New Normal

The following is an excerpt from

The Outside, Book 4...

Day 15

I walked down the aisle in the October sunshine. My hair pins didn't hurt so much anymore, and the veil wasn't so irritating. I felt my two-foot train dragging behind me, along with the stares of the hundreds of friends and family that had come to witness such a blessed day. My heart that had only moments before been pounding at a thousand beats per minute had calmed to a slower pace.

I hadn't realized how completely ready I was for this day. The man waiting at the end of the aisle wasn't just the love of my life. He was my best friend and my soul mate. I'd known this for quite some time, and I was so happy it was finally time to make things official.

My skin glowed, and I felt prettier than I'd ever felt before. This day could not have been more perfect. My mother and Ryan's mother were watching proudly, with smiles on their faces and tears in their eyes. My gaze swept the crowd. But then I focused on my best friend, the man of my dreams, my soon-to-be partner in life. Ryan.

The aisle seemed too long, and the beat to the wedding anthem seemed much too slow. The closer I got to Ryan, the happier I felt. The idea of spending forever with him was no longer too hard to imagine. It now felt completely right. We'd conquered everything together; there was nothing we couldn't do. As I reached him, I realized I was finally ready for this. No more fear. No more questioning. Only excitement for what was to come. Our future. He held out his hand to me. When I placed my hand in his, with it I also placed my body, heart, and soul.

...For more, get your copy of
The Outside, Book 4 today!